MW00874128

This is a work of fiction. Names, characters, businesses, places, events and incidents are either the products of the author's imagination or used in a fictitious manner. Any resemblance to actual persons, living or dead, or actual events is purely coincidental.

Behaettin, Filiz

Henry the Strange Bee.

ISBN 978-0-6489476-0-8

Henry the Strange Bee

Written by Filiz Behaettin
Illustrated by Maryna Kryvets

The honeybees all looked the same.
Yet amongst them, was a rather different looking bee. His name was Henry.
Not only did Henry look different, but he acted differently too. Henry flew around in zigzags.
And he didn't make a buzzing sound like the other bees; Henry made trumpet sounds instead.

All the other bees loved Henry, all except for Mr. Fuzzy Grumpy.
Mr. Fuzzy Grumpy was a mean, grumpy bee who would make fun of Henry.
All the bees were scared of Mr. Fuzzy Grumpy, including Henry.
"You're not a proper bee Henry; you make trumpet sounds and have bright stripes."
"Zigzag away and let the real bees work!" he yelled.

Henry was sad.
"Why don't I look like the other bees?" he thought to himself.

The next day, Henry flew away.
As he was flying, he saw a large mud puddle.
"I've had enough of these bright stripes."

Sad and upset, Henry began rolling around in the mud.

Just at that moment, something caught his eye. It was a large daisy flower!

"I'm going to be like the other bees!"

Henry flew straight into the bright yellow centre of the flower.

"Now, to prove to Mr. Fuzzy Grumpy, I am a proper bee!"
Henry began to fly home when he heard a faint sound.
"Help, help, help!"

As Henry flew closer, he could see a big spider
getting ready to have his dinner!

Henry zigzagged into action.

"Too-too-too-too-tooooooooommmmmm!"

BOOOOMMMMMM

"It's okay Mr. Fuzzy Grumpy, you can open your eyes, he's gone!"

All the other bees had arrived just in time.
"Who are you?" asked Mr. Fuzzy Grumpy and the other bees.

"Who am I!?"

"HENRY!!!" yelled all the bees in excitement.
Mr. Fuzzy Grumpy couldn't believe his eyes.

"Ohh Henry I'm terribly sorry"
"If it wasn't for your trumpet sounds and zigzagging, I would have been eaten alive!"
"I'm sorry for being mean because you were different."

"That's okay Mr. Fuzzy Grumpy. I guess being different isn't so bad after all."
"No, it isn't Henry. Now get rid of that silly disguise, I much prefer the real Henry."

From that day on, Henry proudly showed off his bright stripes, trumpeted loudly, flew in zigzags and realised nothing was wrong with being different.

CPSIA information can be obtained
at www.ICGtesting.com
Printed in the USA
BVHW020937091120
592840BV00004B/29

Batch 592840BV00004B						
592840BVX00029B	9780648947622	Henry the Strange Bee				
COLORCASE	8.00X8.00	20	<AAA>	0.25	GLOSS	(1)
592840BVX00030B	9780615343570	Nursies When the Sun Shines: A Little Bo				
COLORCASE	8.00X8.00	18	<AAA>	0.25	MATTE	(2)

Promise Date: 10-NOV-20 (TUE) Promise Date: 10-NOV-20 (TUE)

592840BV00004B/24

INGRAM:COLORPREMIUM

COLORCASE

592840BVX00029B - 592840BVX00030B [2 : 3]

* 5 9 2 8 4 0 B V 0 0 0 0 4 B *

BOOK
PRCO7019 CONTAINS: COLOR

MIXED

Department Operator's Name (Please print)

Printing ____________________

Binding ____________________

Cutting ____________________

Shipping ____________________

Batch Location ____________________